P9-DDC-114

In memory of Elizabeth Tamara Angelique Spencer
May 29, 2010 – December 10, 2015 ~ T. C. x

For my nephew Jonah, and all our Christmases to come! x
~ T. W.

tiger tales
5 River Road, Suite 128, Wilton, CT 06897
Published in the United States 2017
Originally published in Great Britain 2017
by Little Tiger Press
Text copyright © 2017 Tracey Corderoy
Illustrations copyright © 2017 Tim Warnes
Visit Tim Warnes at www.ChapmanandWarnes.com
ISBN-13: 978-1-68010-067-9
ISBN-10: 1-68010-067-X
Printed in China
LTP/1400/1815/0217

All rights reserved
10 9 8 7 6 5 4 3 2 1

For more insight and activities, visit us at www.tigertalesbooks.com

It's Christmas!

by Tracey Corderoy

Illustrated by Tim Warnes

dinosaurs
blocks
sled!
digger
rocket

tiger tales

Christmas was coming,
and Otto was excited.
More excited than **EVER!**

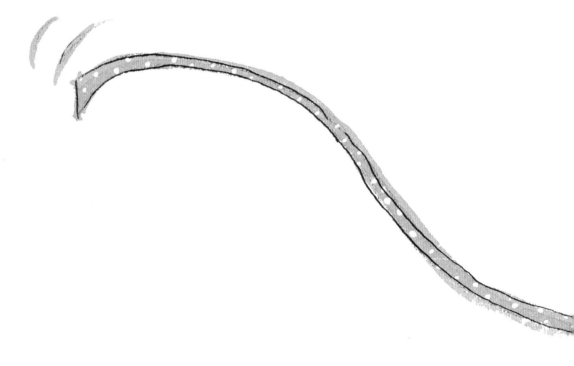

Dad's Christmas cookies smelled yummy.

But Otto wanted to make them
even better.

They're not **Christmassy** enough!

So he plopped on more icing and covered them with **LOTS** of sprinkles.

"Look, Dad!" said Otto.

"Christmas penguins!"

Next, Otto helped Mom decorate the tree. But the new decorations weren't quite right . . . .

Those aren't **Christmassy** enough!

So Otto found the old ones instead.

Ooo!

Sparkly!

He even found the star
that **NEVER** stopped flashing!
"Now it really feels like Christmas!"
Otto smiled.

Ding Dong! went the doorbell.

It was Grandma and Grandpa in their colorful Christmas sweaters!

Otto looked down at his sweater and sighed.

It's not **Christmassy** enough!

So out came his craft box, and Otto got busy . . . .

"Ta-daa!" Otto beamed, and he spun around.

"Watch the tree!" Grandpa cried as it

wibbled and
wobbled
and . . .

"Hmmm," said Mom. "I wonder . . .
who would like a **VERY** Christmassy job?"

Mom sat Otto down by the window.
"I need you to watch . . . for snow,"
she whispered.

"Yay!" cheered Otto.
"Snow is **SUPER**-Christmassy!"

Otto waited, and **waited**, and **WAITED**.

But the snow didn't come.

Not

one

flake.

This isn't Christmassy at **ALL!**

Even Tiger looked sad.

But then Otto had a great idea . . . .

"Oh, Otto!" sighed Dad. "All of the presents are buried in snow!"

So Otto swept the snow off the presents.
But—**OOPS!**—he swept the labels off, too!

Where did each one GO?

By Christmas morning, everything felt perfectly Christmassy —there was even REAL snow!

"Time to open presents!" Mom called. They all gathered around. But—**oh, no**— something wasn't quite right.

Dad had Grandma's balls of yarn,
Mom had Grandpa's fishing pole,
Grandma had Dad's drum set,
and Otto had Mom's
favorite perfume!

Then Grandpa opened the best present of all . . . .

Luckily, Mom fixed everything.

But Grandma loved Dad's drums so much,
they let her bang out one more Christmas
carol. Now even Otto had to agree . . .

. . . that this was the most Christmassy Christmas **EVER!**